"*Effie breathes life into death in a way most authors can only dream of. Her words drip with pure poetic imagery, dancing circles around the reader in ways that make this a truly magical experience.*"

–*Nathaniel Luscombe*
(Author of *Moon Soul* and *The Planets We Become*)

A Gothic Anthology About Bones, Magic, and Grief

BLEACHED REMINDERS

Effie Joe Stock

DRAGON BONE

PUBLISHING™

To all the animals I've loved in life and in death,

&

To those who feel the weight of bones and the lives they once held.

CONTENTS

FOREWORD

Skulls and bones have always held a very special place in my heart and this anthology is my ode to that. Each story and poem are an aspect of the importance I feel bones and death have in our lives whether to act as closure for death, or to offer a memory of life. Bones and skulls are magnificent works of art, too often shunned by society and diminished before anyone can properly experience their worth and morbid beauty.

Each piece in this anthology holds a bit of fantasy and a bit of truth, along with a very gentle whisper to remind you that you are never truly alone, not even when faced with death.

—*Effie Joe Stock*

BLEACHED REMINDERS

Effie Joe Stock

SACRIFICE ROCK

The wind twists from east to west and kisses my wispy cheeks with a familiar whisper. *"She's coming."* I turn to follow the calling—a familiar tug I know too well and have never bothered to resist.

An aching silence devours the air in place of crunching leaves as my feet pad across the autumn blanketed ground. It's been so long since they've crunched for me, so long since the forest snapped and crackled in response to my physical touch. A smile creeps across my face as I watch a squirrel scurry from its tree to the ground, oblivious to my presence, its little paws making such a ruckus in the trees' last clothes of the year.

Knots in my stomach tighten in excitement, then flutter still as the calling grows stronger. *I wonder who she will bring to me this time?* A chill rushes past my legs as the wispy form of a baby goat bounds past me, kicking its dainty little feet—hooves that never got the chance to carry the little goat through life, or crunch through fallen leaves. Not a sound was heard by the living forest as the goat bleated and knickered, waiting only a moment for me to catch up.

My chuckles ringing through the red, orange, and yellow cloaked trees like wind through a chime, I scoop the little goat into my arms, feeling neither warmth nor its softness on my skin. It wouldn't feel me either, I knew. Strange how we could be so close to one another, and yet so far.

"Come, little one. Let us see who she brings to us today."

We step out of the woods onto an old road which had been beaten too well into the forest floor for it to give in to the wild just yet, and I catch sight of the girl whose weeping had called my soul to hers.

"Here she is. See who she has brought you," the wind whispers to me again.

I follow the girl until she reaches the small bluff that overlooks the dark expanse of the forest. With shaking legs, she kneels to the dirt, unaware that her nice jeans will now be stained from the moist, decomposing leaves.

If I still had a physical heart, it would have lurched in my chest as I watch her.

Gently, as if the poor animal can still feel something, she lowers the unmoving body of a white and black cat to the large, flat, empty rock.

"Sacrifice Rock," I whisper, repeating the name this girl had given the rock the first time she had brought to my forest the still form of an animal she had once loved.

The little goat squirms out of my arms as I kneel in front of the girl. He bounds to her side and prances around her, nibbling on her clothes, and nuzzling her cheek. She doesn't know he is here; she doesn't know that she isn't alone. Yet, as if it were yesterday, I remember her whispering his name for the last time when she had brought his small, motionless body to Sacrifice Rock. "Tango," I whisper it again as he lays by her side.

Placing my hand on the cat's soft fur, I wait to

hear what she calls it.

For a long time, all the forest echoes back are the girl's quiet sobs. She tries to wipe the tears from her eyes, tries to smother the pain her heart is crying out, but no matter how much she tries, she cannot stop this ache in her chest—love with nowhere else to go now that the creature she loved has died.

Moving closer to her, I wrap my arm around her. She cannot see me, nor can she feel me, just as she is unaware of Tango at her other side, bleating at her and nibbling the distress in her jeans. But I wish to believe that somehow her heart is comforted by my promise to watch over this creature she has loved.

"It's alright, sweet girl. It's alright to cry. It's alright to love. It's alright to ... let go."

She takes a shaking breath, presses her lips to the cat's soft fur, brushes her fingers across the little pale nose as if the cat is only sleeping, and whispers her name to the wind, letting it carry the word into the forest. "Stardust."

Though I've not cried a single tear since the day I woke up in the forest, an unseen, unheard, and forgotten shepherd of lost things, I still feel my heart aching alongside hers with the all too familiar pain of losing something you know you can never get back.

But when she whispers the rest of the words she needs to say the most, a new emotion takes root in her grieving soul—relief.

"Goodbye, Stardust."

I kiss the girl's forehead just before she stands. "I promise I'll take good care of her," I whisper.

Then, as she says a prayer to the God she is devoted to, thanking Him for the little life she had loved for not nearly long enough, I press my lips to the cat's ear and whisper the words the forest once whispered to me so many years ago.

"Wake up."

Wispy eyes blinking open, the cat slowly takes to her feet, stretches, and yawns, leaving her physical body behind, and joining me in this quiet sanctuary in the forest.

"Say goodbye, Stardust." I gently push the cat toward the girl.

As the girl turns to walk away, the cat meows and purrs, rubbing herself against her legs. She is pleading for one last pet, one last touch, one last kiss that I know will never come.

The leaves crunching under her feet, the girl trudges back up the hill, disappearing down the road from which she came.

"Goodbye for now, sweet girl," I whisper, though I know she will never hear me. "I will see you again." I smile sadly as Tango and Stardust stop following the girl. Ceasing their pitiful cries for her to return to them, they finally turn back to me.

Though I don't know what drove her to bring the first beloved animal to Sacrifice Rock only a few years ago, I believe the forest brought us together, knowing my lonely heart needed her the same way her grief needed me. I know this just as I know that though her heart will always resent death, and never forget little Stardust, deep down, her soul has found some peace, knowing that I am here to take care of all the little creatures she has brought me and the forest to care for.

Picking up Tango and calling for Stardust to follow, I slowly drift back into the woods, letting the wind push me back into autumn spotted branches where tens of other passed on animals wait for me. Lambs, goats, chickens, ducks, and dogs—each a creature she had raised and loved, and then, in the stillness of their death, had brought back to the forest, to where they will live on eternally under my watch, safe in the arms of the trees, knowing no pain, or fear, or sorrow.

And one day, the girl's heart will heal, and she will learn to love again. Then, when it is time for another creature to pass on, she will bring their precious form to the forest and I will meet her again, to take into my arms whoever else she brings to me at Sacrifice Rock.

Bleached Reminders

Speak softly of death, they say,
If we ignore it enough it'll go away.
But I wonder,
Why are we filled with dismay?

Perhaps we're afraid to be forgotten,
Afraid our memories will be broken,
But we all leave something behind,
Waiting for stories to be spoken.

When all has rotted away,
Pieces of our bodies scattered array,
Bones remain—

Cleaned by nature, free of blight,

Kissed by the sun and bleached clean white.

Pure reminders

Of lives that dimmed with fight.

Gather the bones of the dead to you,

Hold them tenderly and remember their value,

And listen gently,

To what they leave in residue.

"I lived. I lived. I lived."

They cry. Their words, once adrift,

Now whisper to you,

Reminding you why you exist,

And how you will not be forgotten,

When you at last taste death's kiss.

THE SOUL-FILLED SKULLS OF EPSIE REES

From the moment Epsie Rees was born under a moon-less sky on Halloween night with the marking of a white wolf skull upon her dark forehead, the coven knew she would be different. Perhaps the lack of her cries filling the autumn air also alluded them to this, or the way her wide yellow eyes seemed to glow with their own l

"No witch has ever been born on a moonless night before, at least not one from our coven. She's an anomaly." Their High Priestess crossed her arms, her long black nails tapping impatiently.

"No, she is blessed." Tears gathered in Epsie Rees's mother's eyes as she brushed the little babe's white hair from her solemn face. "Her mark," the woman's fingers brushed across the wolf birthmark on Epsie

Rees's dark forehead, "is a sign of companionship, of loyalty."

The Priestess's blue eyes narrowed. "It could also be a sign of danger, of destruction. A witch born on Halloween is not to be taken lightly. Whatever powers she will possess will be enhanced by our moon goddess's blessing. True, she may be loyal, but she may also be a threat."

"Please, High Priestess. She is only a babe. We've been so dedicated to the order, you know this. We've given our life to our coven, and we are willing to give hers as well. We do not yet know what she will grow to be, but please give her and us a chance."

The father, Ganon, was kneeling next to his wife, eyes pleading with their leader. He and his wife had black hair, which made Epsie Rees's white hair all the more unique and strange.

For a long, aching moment, their leader said nothing, then reached for the babe. With shaking hands, Epsie Rees's mother handed her daughter to the High Priestess who took off her hat and passed it to a demure witch in a long, dark green cloak.

Gently, she held the baby, staring deep into her gaze. "Epsie Rees," she whispered. "Why has the moon sent you?" Long black nails touched the babe's head but without fear, Epsie Rees only giggled and reached her small, dark hands to hold one of the witch's fingers. Blinking in shock, the High Priestess wrapped her slender fingers around Epsie's little hand, feeling the life of the moon within her touch. "Very well then."

Epsie Rees's parents cried in relief as their daughter was handed back to them, safely wrapped in their arms. The Priestess's familiar, stoic expression returned, her pointed, mouse skull decorated hat covering her fiery red hair once again.

"I welcome Epsie Rees into the world under the laws and protection of our coven and our moon goddess." Her handmaiden witches bowed low; their arms linked beneath the sweeping sleeves of their cloaks.

"But I warn you, Endora and Ganon." The High Priestess's face darkened, the black tattoos across her skin seeming to grow with the shadow in her eyes. "If she expresses any violence toward our coven and is a toxic omen of any kind, I will deem her life to have been born as a sacrifice to the moon and she will be eliminated from our coven immediately. Do you understand?"

The new parents barely nodded; their joy was too great to be dampened by the dark words of their leader as they gazed into the now laughing face of their newborn baby.

Though the threat was never forgotten, it wasn't until much later that the strangeness of Epsie Rees became the coven's problem.

"She's just a late bloomer! She's hardly normal, I mean look at her. How many humans do you think play with bones like that?" Endora gestured wildly to the little white-haired girl on the forest floor, a rabbit skull in one hand and the foot of a crow in the other.

"Four years old is longer than a late bloomer. That's just a dud." The man stepped forward menacingly, his bare chest rising and falling with anger. This wasn't the first time they'd come to test Epsie

Rees's magic capabilities, and it wasn't the first time they'd seen her magicless. "A little girl raised in a witch coven is bound to play with bones. That's hardly an indication of the witch blood inside her. She hasn't expressed any magic yet, and she's not likely to."

Tears filled Endora's eyes as she scooped her daughter into her arms. "Please. She was born on Halloween, she has the hair of the moon, the mark of a wolf familiar on her forehead. That alone is enough signs that she is of the witch blood. My family heritage goes back hundreds of years; our blood is strong and pure. There must be another explanation for this, one that we don't know yet."

He raised his hand to Epsie, his long, navy-blue nails scrapping her soft dark skin; she didn't cry, only stared at him with large yellow eyes. "She was born to be a sacrifice to the moon. If the moon goddess does not taste the blood sacrifice she gave us, she will grow angry." He wrapped his ring decorated hand around Epsie Rees's head and squeezed ever so slightly. Rage burned in Endora's eyes but they both knew she wasn't high enough in the coven to defy his authority.

"I will decide who and what is to be offered as sacrifice for our goddess. We are not barbarians, Draco. One thousand years have passed since the coven offered a witch or human's blood to the moon goddess. She is not a goddess of death or violence. Watch what you say, or I'll banish you to a coven that will gladly sever your head for their own bloodthirsty gods."

Snarling, Draco released his hold on Epsie Rees and bowed low, his long tunic sweeping the forest floors.

"Begone from us." The High Priestess waved her hand to dismiss him. With one last glare at Endora, he disappeared into the darkness of the trees, autumn leaves crunching under his boots.

Once the forest was still again, only the wind rustling the leaves as a crow cawed in the distance, the High Priestess turned to the mother. "You know what our coven must do to those who do not have magic?" Her face held an unusual amount of compassion.

The defensiveness in Endora faded into sorrow. "I know. I understand why our coven doesn't take lightly to the magicless. I know it's to defend ourselves. But Epsie Rees is a full blood witch, she shouldn't have trouble accessing her magic. I just don't understand why it hasn't manifested yet." She stared at her daughter who was reaching for the High Priestess. To Endora's surprise, the leader took the young girl into her arms and let her reach for her hat.

Taking off her hat, they watched as Epsie Rees immediately reached for the mouse skulls, her little giggles filling the autumn quiet of the forest.

"The only time I see her smile and laugh is when she's holding a skull. I've never figured out why. She doesn't laugh with the other babies, or when I play peek-a-boo with her, and she despises all other toys."

The Priestess grunted as she pulled her hat from Epsie's hands. "It's certainly unusual, but like Draco said, it's not uncommon. I would be more surprised if she *didn't* like skulls. To be honest ..." she sighed heavily as if weighing whether or not she should say what was on her mind. "I'm fond of Epsie Rees. I think there's a reason she was born on Halloween with the markings she has. I believe she has some connection to the moon goddess that we have yet to find out."

Endora nodded quickly as she took her daughter back, setting her on the forest floor so she could play with her bones once again, oblivious to her fate being decided above her. "That's what I believe too. I know it must be true. I think—"

"Endora, but if she doesn't show signs of magic by the time she is thirteen-years-old, we will have to treat her as any other magicless. Do you understand?"

Endora's mouth shut, tears welling up in her eyes. Sniffing and trying to compose herself, adjusting her pointed, feather decorated hat and gripping her skirts in white knuckled hands, Endora quickly nodded. "I understand. I know she'll pass the tests. I know she's a witch. She must be."

"We shall see."

Before the High Priestess walked away, Endora whispered under her breath. "You know I am loyal to the coven; you know I love them and will give my life for them."

"I know."

"But High Priestess ..." She paused, the words catching in her throat, heart racing in her chest. "I love my daughter so much more and I will do anything, *anything* to protect her."

A long silence passed between them until the High Priestess nodded. "I know."

"Ew, get away from us, you magicless human!"

The words stung Epsie Rees like the bite of a wasp, or a rat caught in a trap. Flinching from the other witches as they waved their arms, trying to scare her off, she forced a smile onto her face. "I'm not a human," she whispered so meekly she was certain her familiar would be a mouse rather than the wolf that marked her forehead.

"Epsie Rees, listen." One of the older teen witches pushed her way through the children, kneeling down to face the thirteen-year-old. "We know your parents are witches, but some of our ancestors had affairs with the magicless and sometimes that comes out in us. It wouldn't be ... unheard of for you to be magicless."

Espie Rees could hardly force herself to look into

the shinning green eyes of the witch before her. She admired Narcissa since she was one of the few young witches who would even talk to her. She also envied the way her dark hair was so typical of witches, and the way her pale skin shone like the bones they used in their potions; but though Epsie Rees's dark skin wasn't uncommon, her mother had dark skin and so did one of the coven leaders, pale skin was much more typical and accepted.

"But Mama says we're pure bloods." Epsie Rees sniffed, wiping her nose on the back of her tattered robe sleeve in the way she knew her mother despised. Her little yellow eyes darted off to the woods beyond where she saw the flicker of blue mist. "And I have magic. I see animals. I see them in their eyes."

Narcissa smiled sadly as she softly touched Epsie Rees's arm. "You say that, Epsie Rees, but no one knows what you're saying."

A knot tightened in her stomach as the chill of the coming winter's air blew across her ankles, making her wish she'd worn her long stockings with the purple and black stripes. "But—"

"You're making excuses." Another witch stood

20

over Narcissa, arms crossed, a sneer across her black painted lips, her already dark eyes drowning in the black makeup she'd rimmed them with, her dark brown hair trailing down off her shoulders in two braids.

"Now, Sabrina, don't say things like that. We don't know—"

Sabrina spat on the ground by Epsie Rees and flicked one of her braids off her shoulder. "We do know, Narcissa. Each witch is sorted into their respective talents: alchemy, necromancy, earth, stars, or spiritual energies. Nothing more. Never before has a witch had magic that didn't fit into one of those categories. It simply isn't possible."

Narcissa opened her mouth, then closed it again, standing slowly. Nothing was left to be said. They all knew it was true.

"I can't believe they haven't kicked you out yet. You're a disgrace. I bet your father was a human. I bet that's why he's not around anymore. They probably found him out and kicked him out too."

Tears spilled down Epsie Rees's night black cheeks

but the only feeling that stirred inside her was an empty numbness.

"Sabrina," Narcissa hissed warningly. "That's enough."

"Well, it's true."

It wasn't, but Epsie Rees couldn't find the words to defend herself or her family.

"Go on with the others, Sabrina."

Sabrina sneered and shook her head before picking her broom up and straddling it, flying off to the tops of the trees where the other witches waited, mocking the outcast.

"Don't listen to them." Narcissa placed her hand on Epsie Rees's shoulder. "I know you'll pass your test well enough; then they'll see that you're as much a witch as we are."

They both knew she was wrong.

When Sabrina didn't get a response, she turned slightly, her shoulders sagging as she waved her hand, her broom jumping up to meet her fingers. "Why don't you go home, Epsie Rees? I'm sure your mother needs help with dinner."

They both knew she didn't.

But Epsie Rees had no choice. Without magic, her broom sat at home propped up in a corner, collecting dust between the days she used it to sweep the floor—a disgrace to what the broom was capable of.

"Okay." She forced the word out of her mouth but when she tried to raise her lips with a smile to match, they only quivered and grew wet with the tears that danced from her eyes.

Narcissa mounted her broom, pausing for a moment as if she wanted to say something, or perhaps she was waiting for Epsie Rees to say something.

They were both disappointed.

In the aching silence that filled the rustling autumn air, Narcissa pushed off from the ground and flew effortlessly into the sky, her friends only waiting a moment before they all flew off into the fiery orange and pink sky.

Epsie Rees wrapped her arms around herself, mindlessly picking at one of her broken nails. Her mother had just painted them dark red this morning and she'd spent the last few months growing them out for her thirteenth birthday. Would her mother be upset that she broke it off? Or would she understand that she hadn't meant to when the other witches had shoved her to the ground, and she'd barely caught herself before her face met the dirt?

But a nail was a small thing to worry about with her birthday coming up. Over the years, her mother had become more and more frenzied about her manifesting magic. She'd taken her to the sacred moon priestesses in the late of night to perform sacrifices, drink potions, pray to the goddess, undergo horrifying hypnosis, pain treatments—anything they could think of—to somehow trigger the magic. None of it had worked. At least, not according to the adults in her life.

Epsie Rees turned back to the forest where she had seen the wispy blue mist. The bush rustled, and the snap of a twig alerted her to the little life. Brushing away her tears and remembering who her real friends were, Epsie Rees sneaked close to the foliage, quiet as a mouse.

"Boo!" She jumped around the bush, laughing as the little fox startled and jumped high before he yipped and ran circles around her feet, licking her ankles, and wiggling his little body in joy.

Laughter trilling through the red, orange, and yellow trees, Epsie Rees knelt to hug the fox, the little wispy licks from his tongue tickling her face. When she wrapped her arms around him to carry him with her, she felt no soft fur, nor the weight of it. After all, he wasn't a living fox ... he was a ghost.

Skipping through the quiet forest, Epsie Rees watched the trees and little bird ghosts jumped from branch to branch, following a path only she knew, a path leading her safely around all the other witches' cottages.

Once they were deep in the forest, where the trees grew crooked and had black bark and dark red leaves, Epsie Rees let the fox jump to the ground before pushing aside the branches she had stacked against the front of her little cave.

The entrance was small and dark, the only light she could see coming from just up ahead or from the little mice and snake ghosts scurrying around her feet, rushing to the inside of the cave. After squeezing past the last jut of rock in the tunnel, she was once again in her own personal sanctuary.

A deep breath entered her lungs, filling her soul with renewed joy and peace before she took in what she had spent so many years building.

The cavern was lit up by large splits in the rock above her; light from the sunset spilled into the cave, scattering when it reflected off the many mirrors she had positioned to enhance the moon's light when it decided to shine. With painstaking effort, she had carved shelves and nooks into the cave walls. And upon all those rock ledges sat the soul-filled skulls of Epsie Rees.

"Hello, friends." A smile cracked her black lips as she stared back into the empty eye sockets of the motionless skulls. Taking off her hat and hanging it on a nail she'd driven into the rock by the entrance, Epsie Rees sat down in the center of the cavern, telling the silent skulls all about her day, about the horrible things the other witches had said to her, about how she couldn't fly off with them and had to walk everywhere instead. Tears dripped from her eyes, down her sharp cheeks and tangled in her thick, curly white hair, cold next to her skin.

"They don't believe me when I say I can see you."

The little wispy fox crawled into her lap, yipping, and barking as he flopped onto his back so she would rub his tummy. "They don't believe me when I say they destroy a soul every time they crush the skulls for their potions."

Staring into her eyes, the fox looked as if he could speak, if only he could find the words. Though the words never left his snout, she knew what he was saying.

"I know, but the skulls make their potions more powerful. Otherwise, I don't think they'd mind letting me collect the skulls. Why do you think I had to make this cave to keep all of you hidden? If only they knew the power came from your very lives, maybe they'd be willing to give up some of that power."

Eyes wandering the skull-filled cave, she let a deep sigh escape her lips. Slowy, the skulls began to glow a sky-blue aura that slipped out of the mouths, eye sockets, and brain stems of the skulls, collecting over them and forming into the shapes of animals. They hoped down from the shelves and jumped around the cave, playing, or wrestling with each other. A little goat bound over to Epsie Rees, nibbling on her hair, though her hair mostly just passed through the misty ethereal manifestation of its soul. Laughing, she scratched the little goat on the side of her neck just as she liked, though Epsie Rees felt only cold air instead of warm fur.

Each skull she found in the forest and brought here was full of the essence of the animal who had once lived inside of it. As long as the skull was still mostly intact, the little creature's life would linger on, able to play with their friends or run free through the forest. If their skulls were left to decay, the animals' spirits would pass on into the cosmos and become one again with the universe. But if they were crushed and used in the witches' potions and spells, their essence would be used to power the magic and not only would the little soul disappear, but so would its chance of living on in the stars and in the world around them.

It seemed impossible to make the other witches understand. As the only witch who could see the souls in the animal skulls, it not only made Espie Rees seem magicless, but also delusional. No one in her thirteen years of life had believed her when she'd spoken of the souls. Except for maybe her mother, but if Endora truly believed her daughter possessed a unique magic, would she have done all she had to awaken typical magic in Epsie Rees?

The question left a gaping hole inside Epsie Rees as another tear rolled from her cheek. She would stay here a few more hours since she'd convinced her mother the other witches liked her and let her join them doing whatever the 'regular' witches did. Of course, it was only a lie to ease her mother's fears and most of the nights, as long as she was able to escape the brutal verbal and sometimes physical assaults of the other witches or the experimental rituals they often performed on her, she came here to spend the hours until sunset.

Lying down, she felt the cold little ghost bodies of all her animal friends gathering around her: goats, coyotes, cats, birds, mice, foxes, bats, even a pig who curled up at her back. A little mouse snuggled into her thick hair and a bird perched on her shoulder.

The little baby goat she'd named Jasmine nibbled on her ankle, eyes pleading for her to come play with the other goats and sheep as they bound out of the cave. But Epsie Rees's very tired little eyes had already shut, and she was fast asleep.

"Epsie Rees! What on earth are you doing? Do you realize how bad this looks? We're late!"

Epsie Rees sat up with a startled gasp, heart pounding in her chest. Dreams of her father being present for her thirteenth birthday still grasped at the edges of her mind and a heavy cloud settled on her when reality crashed down on her. The sorrow in her heart over her deceased father gathered and mingled with the dread of what today would bring.

But no time was left for grieving or worrying. Her mother was hauling her off the cold stone floor, cursing the skulls and all Epsie Rees's absentmindedness.

Epsie Rees turned one last time to see all the little ghost animals sitting around the cave, eyes pleading for her to stay, to never walk into the day where the other witches waited for her to fail her test and put her on trial for conspiracy against the coven. But as much as she wished she could stay hidden with the animals forever, she couldn't. Eventually she would be found, and her fate would be the same. She couldn't escape this.

Was this the last time she would see her friends? Or would her soul stay behind after her execution to live amongst the forest and the only creatures who ever truly cared about her?

"We don't have time to fix your clothes. Goddess, help me, you look like you're homeless."

"I basically am," Epsie Rees muttered under her breath, but her mother only cast her a dark glance before prattling on for the millionth time what the trials would demand of her.

A knife twisted in Epsie Rees's heart. When had her mother become so harsh and loveless? When had the pressure of the coven gotten in the way of them loving and caring for each other? Even if she miraculously manifested the typical witch magic the coven expected of her, would she be able to repair the damage between her mother and her? Would it all have been different if her father had lived to this day?

With a harsh preening and a few hurried spells, her mother was able to make her hair less tangled, her dark makeup less smeared and her clothes less wrinkled, though her dress still smelled like cave must and her shoes were still wet from the morning forest dew and decomposition.

In less time than Epsie Rees would've wished, they were in the center of their coven where all their ritual circles were drawn. The entire coven was present to witness her trials and all hopes of running away dissolved into the increasingly inescapable fate she saw playing out before her.

The High Priestess in her flowing robes stood in the center of them all. They didn't have a stage or platform for anyone to speak on, even their High Priestess, for they believed they were all equal under the moon goddess and that pulpits were for the magicless and their strict gods of rules.

"My fellow brothers and sisters under the moon!"

The pointed hats formed a circle around the Priestess and Epsie Rees, Endora having quickly faded into the crowd, maybe because she was ashamed of her magicless daughter, or maybe just because parents weren't allowed. Epsie Rees wouldn't know either way; she'd never been allowed to attend any of their rituals before.

The High Priestess continued with her speech, a few of the witches in the crowd shouting slander at Epsie Rees occasionally, but the young witch was focused on only one thing: the little mice ghosts running around the High Priestess's hat rim, unable to leave because their skulls were tied so tightly to the thick fabric.

With pleading eyes, the little ghosts squeaked at her, begging to be released. Tears filled Epsie Rees's eyes as she choked back the emotion. If she didn't pass this trial, and she knew wouldn't, she would no longer be here to protect the animal ghosts from the horrific fates these clueless witches condemned them to.

The last words of the High Priestess's speech caught her attention. "If Epsie Rees does not pass this trial, I will be forced to deem her magicless and therefore a threat to the coven, after which she would be put on trial and dealt with accordingly."

Heart pounding, Epsie Rees tried to drown out the jeers of the crowd as they shouted for her to be made a sacrifice to the moon goddess, saying that's all she had been born for.

"Worthless barbarians."

Epsie Rees's eyes widened, thinking maybe she had said the words aloud herself, but when her eyes met the soft gaze of the High Priestess, she was shocked. All her life she had thought the High Priestess despised her. Could she have been wrong? Did that mean she was wrong about her mother too?

Eyes searching the crowd, she found her mother just behind the front row, covered in a dark cloak that matched many of the others around her, a steely look in her eyes, hands ready with magic beneath the long sleeves. She nodded subtly and the High Priestess nodded as well.

Her heart pounded. What was her mother and the High Priestess planning? But it was too late to think about it for the crowd roared in excitement as the High Priestess gathered magic in her hands. Lifting

her arms, she snapped her fingers and a bubbling caul-
dron, a broom, a spell book, potion ingredients, and a
wand appeared on the ground before Epsie Rees.

"Let the trials—"

"Wait!"

The entire crowd fell silent as they turned to the
young witch who had stumbled into the center of the
ritual circle, her dress tattered, hat missing, hair full
of sticks and leaves, and scratches on her face.

For a moment, Epsie Rees thought this was part
of the strange plan her mother and the High Priestess
seemed to have, but when she saw the honest confu-
sion on both their faces, she knew this was entirely
unrelated.

"What's wrong?" The High Priestess caught the
girl as she nearly collapsed at their feet.

Epsie Rees gasped. It was Sabrina.

But it wasn't the High Priestess she wanted to
speak to, it was Epsie Rees.

"Please, you have to find her." Her long-nailed
hands grasped at Epsie Rees's layered skirts, pleading

on her knees, eyes full of tears.

Chaos broke out among the coven as they tried to pull the girl off Epsie Rees and make sense of the situation.

"Who's missing?" The High Priestess's words fell on the girl's ears, but she didn't bat an eye at their leader, instead pleading with Epsie Rees who could only stand frozen, mouth agape, overwhelmed with the chaos.

"Narcissa's lost! We were playing in the woods, preparing our mystic rituals for Halloween night, but when we started to fly back for the trials, Narcissa said she spotted a rare mandrake and wanted to collect it for tonight. We waited for her to come back but she didn't. We searched *everywhere* for her; we tried revealing and tracking spells and nothing worked." The girl was hysterical, sobbing and crying into the arms of those who tried to take her away from Epsie Rees.

Finally, Epsie Rees found her words. "Why did you come to me?" She could barely hear her own voice over the commotion.

"Because you can see the animals, can't you? They know the forest better than anyone, even if they're dead. Please, Epsie Rees. Narcissa told us you can see the animal ghosts. We didn't believe her, but if you can, please. *Please* help her."

Epsie Rees shook her head as the girl was led away, potions passed from witch, to witch, then to her lips as they tried to calm her down and heal her cuts and bruises.

"High Priestess, our search team is ready to find Narcissa." A young witch stepped forward, his belt ladened with potions and his wand, his broom in hand with ten more witches behind him just the same.

The crowd made their support for the search team very clear as they cheered them on and offered extra wands or potions, but the High Priestess raised her hand and quieted them.

"Sabrina came to Epsie Rees and requested her to search for Narcissa."

They roared in disapproval, but their leader quieted them once again. "Epsie Rees has claimed to possess the power to see the souls in the skulls of animals passed on. Either she is telling the truth, or she is lying. This is her new trial. Should she find Narcissa with her own magic, she and her power will be accepted into the coven, but if she fails to find her by midnight tonight, she will be outcast for blasphemy."

They shouted their approval, sure she would fail.

Epsie Rees's eyes met her mother's which held fear, but assuredness. Her mother knew she had never been lying. Now was her chance to prove herself to the coven. Tonight, her fate was not one of death, but one of hope and possibility.

"Thank you, High Priestess." Epsie Rees bowed before her, but she only waved her hand.

"Do not thank me yet. Just get out there, find that girl, and prove that your mother and I are right."

Epsie Rees didn't need to be told twice.

The hours dragged on. Nearly one hundred little animal ghosts were spread through the forest, searching every nook and cranny for the missing girl. Epsie Ree's had even gone into the coven's bone storage rooms and rescued as many skulls as she could carry, much to the anger of the witch in charge of the potion ingredients. Her mother had tried to help her, but the High Priestess stopped her, saying only Epsie Rees could help herself if she was to succeed and win the approval of the coven.

It hadn't even taken a minute of convincing to get the animals to help. All her life they had been waiting for a chance to help her as she had helped them, and to make their existence in the skulls known. Their searching force was greater than all that of the coven combined, but even so, it was nearly nightfall and not even a single shred of witch lace had been found to lead them to Narcissa.

As she sank to the forest floor, the animals gathering around her mournfully, she began to consider the horrible possibility that Narcissa wasn't actually missing, and that this had been an elaborate prank by the young witches to ensure she didn't pass her test. Even though she *could* see the animals, it was no use if Narcissa wasn't actually lost.

The moon was just rising over the treetops, not

quite full, but brighter this Halloween night than it usually was, and Epsie Rees turned her face to it, tears running down her cheeks and neck as she pleaded to her goddess.

"Please, why did you make me? What is my purpose if I am shunned at every turn, if I cannot use real magic, and if the talents I do possess only bring me death? Why did you give me this mark, this mark of danger and companionship if you have given me neither? Please, help me!"

But the moon was cold and silent as it was every other night, as it had been when she had spent hours praying to it, pleading with it to give her magic.

"It's useless."

The animals gathered around her, the little fox and little goat Jasmine curling up next to her, resting their heads in her lap. A crow ghost landed on her shoulder as a few mice snuggled in her hair by her neck. "Should I go back? Or should I walk into the forest and never return?"

The sadness in the fox and Jasmine's eyes was her answer. If she walked away from the coven, she would have to leave all their skulls behind and she would never see them again. She had to stay, even if it meant death, because even if the mark on her forehead hadn't meant companionship from the other witches, she had found her friends in the skulls. They'd never abandoned her, and she wouldn't abandon them.

Taking to her feet, she brushed the tears from her eyes and the dirt and leaves from her dress, threw back her shoulders and took a deep breath. "I will return, find Narcissa in the village, and prove I was set up; if they will not take me after that, then I shall accept death with grace and honor knowing it is better to be dead than to live amongst witches as horrible as they."

But before she could take another step, a crow landed before her in a flutter of black feathers, jumping from one foot to the next, squawking and cawing excitedly.

"You found her."

Epsie Rees took off running after the crow, hardly able to keep up with it. An elk was running next to her and on a leap of faith, praying that somehow the magic would be different on Halloween night, she leapt onto its back, eyes closed, expecting to fall through its blue form and hit the ground.

Instead, she felt the warmth of the animal beneath her, felt its muscles moving and flexing, felt the pounding of the earth beneath her and the fur under her fingers.

Thinking she jumped on a living elk, her eyes snapped open. Instead, she was faced with the unbelievable reality that she was indeed riding on the solid back of a ghost elk. Looking up with tearful eyes, she let the light of the moon wash over her.

"Thank you, goddess."

The forest passed by them in a blur as they wove through the trees, leaping over rocks and logs. Narcissa was farther out than they had anticipated, and Epsie Rees knew that without intricate knowledge of this part of the woods and animals to guide her, she and any other search party wouldn't have been able to find Narcissa.

Epsie Rees knew the exact moment they came into the close vicinity of Narcissa when the air grew dank, and the aura grew darker. Anytime a witch was injured, dark souls would gather to try and take advantage of the physical weakness of the witch so they could capitalize on their spiritual strength.

"Narcissa!" Epsie cupped her hands around her dark lips, calling over and over, waiting to hear something, anything, even a groan. "Search around for her! She can't be far." The animals scattered, sniffing and hunting for the witch. Shadows from the moon grew larger and tendrils of darkness spread from them, also searching for the wounded witch. It was not only a race against the end of her trials at midnight, but also to keep Narcissa from being possessed by the dark souls.

After what was likely only a few minutes but that felt like hours, the fox ran to Epsie Rees, jumping up and down, yipping and barking. The elk loped after the fox as he led them down into a steep ravine. A broken broom stick was shattered on the rocks and dread settled into Epsie Rees's stomach. They'd found Narcissa, but was she still alive? Epsie Rees had to remind herself that the dark souls wouldn't bother themselves with a dead witch. The thought was only slightly comforting.

"Narcissa! Where are you? Are you alright?"

This time a groan answered.

A sheep bleated from the other side of a large rock at the bottom of the ravine. The elk easily picked its way to the bottom where Epsie Rees slid from its back and ran to the motionless girl.

"Narcissa!" She collapsed to the ground next to the witch, ignoring the sharp rocks digging into her knees or the tatters her dress had gathered from the thorns nearby. "Are you alright?" She propped the girl's head up in her lap and brushed her hair from her face, grateful when her eyes flickered open, and she groaned again.

"Epsie Rees? Is that you?"

"Yes, yes, it's me. I found you. The coven is worried sick."

"You came to find me? You care?"

Epsie Ree's heart lurched in her chest as tears rose to her eyes. Despite everything the coven had done to ostracize her, she did, indeed, care very much. "Yes, of course. We witches must stick together, right?"

A smile spread across Narcissa's scratched face. "*We witches.* I like that."

Epsie Rees wasn't sure how to respond, but then didn't have to as she saw Narcissa's leg was twisted in a strange direction. "Your leg is broken." Dread filled her stomach. She didn't know any healing spells and didn't have any healing potions on her. If Narcissa couldn't walk, they'd never get back to the coven by midnight. Panic raced in Epsie Rees's veins as she weighed her options. She could go back to the coven, say she found Narcissa and request help transporting her, but even if they believed she was telling the truth, which she doubted they would, she was sure the High Priestess would once again deny her any help.

A nibble and warm breath on her shoulder startled her and she turned, her nose bumping into the elk. His wide, soft eyes told her everything she needed to know. He was strong enough and big enough to carry them both. And even though Narcissa most likely wouldn't be able to see him, it was worth trying.

"I have an idea to get you back to the coven." She helped the other young witch sit up. "A friend of mine is going to carry us, alright? I just need you to trust me."

Narcissa nodded, eyes rolling into the back of her head. "I trust you, Epsie Rees, I always have."

As Epsie Rees held her up, her arm over her shoulder, Narcissa's eyes fluttered open and focused on the elk.

"Epsie, is that ..." Her voice trailed off as she looked around them, her eyes widening in awe. "The animal ghosts, they're real."

"You—" shock tightened Epsie Rees's chest and she almost dropped the girl. "You can see them?

Narcissa nodded and grinned as the goat nibbled on her dress. "They're beautiful." Her eyes landed on Epsie Rees. "You're beautiful. The moonlight is in your hair."

It wasn't until she said those words that Epsie Rees realized her hair was glowing as white as the moon, reflecting the light onto the ghosts which made them visible to Narcissa.

Words couldn't express how she felt, or what this meant.

"Come on, Narcissa," Epsie Rees whispered through her emotions. "Let's go home."

The midnight hour was nearly upon them. The moon was high in the sky. The coven waited with bated breath. Many of them were excited to see if Epsie Rees would succeed, more hoped she wouldn't. Some were angry that she was put in charge of finding one of their witches and demanded to be allowed to search for Narcissa themselves.

But all fell silent when the underbrush rustled, and Epsie Rees emerged.

All eyes fell first on Epsie Rees, then to the tired injured witch behind her, then to the beast on which they rode. But it wasn't just the elk they saw, it was also every little woodland creature who emerged proudly from the forest and strode into the circle the crowd formed around the High Priestess.

Epsie Rees's mother rushed to the front of the crowd, gasping, hands covering her mouth as she cried tears of relief and joy.

Waiting hands gently removed Narcissa from the elk's back after they hesitantly drew near.

Not a word was spoken by the coven. No doubt was left to harbor.

"Epsie Rees." The High Priestess held her hand out to Epsie Rees as she slid off the back of the elk.

Her heart thundered in her chest as she took the High Priestess's hand, only able to stand on her shaking legs because of the comfort the ghosts around her provided.

"Thank you," the High Priestess whispered.

Epsie Rees's eyes filled with tears as she nodded. She wanted to say more, to thank the High Priestess for her patience, for her justice, mercy, for second chances. But all that came out was a whisper as quiet as a mouse's. "Could you—do mind if I—" she swallowed dryly as the coven leaned forward to hear her words. She pointed to the skulls on the hat. "The mice souls. They can't leave your hat."

Her eyes widened as she looked up at the rim, startled to see a little upside-down mouse peering at her, pleading with its beady eyes. Her gaze met Epsie

Rees's again. "You want me to take the skulls off my hat?"

Epsie Rees felt her face flush red. She broke her eyes from the High Priestess's surprised gaze and nodded slowly. "Just so they can ... be free too. And maybe ..." She couldn't believe the words that were tumbling out of her mouth, but she didn't want to stop them. She was a proved witch of the coven and now that her voice would be listened to, the words rushed out all at once. "Maybe we could stop using the skulls in the potions. It kills the animal's souls when their skulls are crushed up and their life force drained for the magic. I know the potions won't be as strong, but it would save all my friends."

The fox and Jasmine seemed to smile up at her and nod, pride shining in their eyes. She reached out to pet their wispy heads.

Silence gripped the coven.

With every passing second, Epsie Rees became more certain the High Priestess would burst out laughing and brush aside her request.

Then to everyone's surprise, the High Priestess

took off her hat, ripped mice skulls from the thread-ing of the fabric, and delicately handed them to Epsie Rees. With excited squeaks, the little mice ghosts ran from the Priestess's hands to Epsie Rees's and then into her hair.

"I hereby declare that no animals' skulls are ever to be used in destructive rituals or potions. From here on out, all animal skulls will go into the protection and care of Epsie Rees."

Then with warm arms, the High Priestess em-braced the young witch whose eyes filled with tears, too shocked to move, even to hug her back. "Welcome to the coven."

The crowd erupted in cheers and little explosions of magic declared their celebration.

Epsie Rees's mother grasped her hands, tears pour-ing down her face, dragging her dark eye makeup with it.

"Mother ..."

Endora shook her head, throwing her arms around her daughter. "Oh Epsie Rees ..."

Epsie Rees tried to swallow her tears. "I'm a part of the coven now. You don't have to worry about me failing the trials anymore. You don't have to worry about me not being a witch."

Her mother drew away from her, cupping her face in her hands, searching her eyes. "Oh, Epsie Rees. I never once doubted you were a witch. Not once. And did you really think I'd let you fail the trials?" She looked over her shoulder as the High Priestess winked at them, nodding to her mother and her.

Epsie Rees laughed, her suspicions confirmed.

"But you didn't need me, not like I thought you did. You're your own witch, Epsie Rees. You only ever needed to be true to yourself." Endora tucked a thick curl of daughter's shining white hair behind her ear, giggling when a little mouse ghost ran across her finger.

"Does that mean you're proud of me?"

Endora's eyes shone. "I have *always* been proud of you, my little witch. *Always*." She embraced her daughter again, rocking her back and forth. "And if you'll have me, I would love to help you care for all the skulls and all the little souls inside of them."

Epsie hugged her mother even tighter. "I would love nothing more than that."

ACKNOWLEDGEMENTS

I want to give a special "thank you" to all the amazing people in my life, mainly my closest friends and family, who have always supported me for who I am, including my morbid interest in death and bones.

And how could I write a book about them without thanking all the animals who have loved me and cared for me, many of which I did indeed take to sacrifice rock to give them back to the forest. Tango, Star Dust, and Jasmine are all animals I love in life and in death and they, along with so many more, have taught me the most about love and grief.

A kind remembrance and thank you to whoever Epsie Rees was, from whose tombstone I gathered the name for my own stories. May you rest in sweet peace.

Thank you, reader, for picking up this beautiful little book and stepping into the world of bones and skulls that I call home.

Remember, no matter what you do in life, no matter your choices, your appearance, your beliefs, someday all that's left will be bones. Take comfort in that, for there is beauty even in the simplicity of death.

—*Effie Joe Stock*